L.T. GRUNDY

Blood In The Eye Of The Storm

Killer Instincts - Book 3

First edition

This book was professionally typeset on Reedsy.
Find out more at reedsy.com

Contents

Subscribe Now For Exclusive Content

Stay In Touch With LT To Receive Book Updates and Offers!

Sign up for my newsletter HERE
You can also join our ARC team HERE

Get in touch with L.T. by email at LTGrundyBooks@gmail.com

Subscribe now for exclusive updates, promos, giveaways, and updates on the next book!

1

One

A smile formed on the edge of her mouth, looking at the blazing sunshine on the horizon. It wasn't easy to leave all of her worries behind for parts unknown in Jamaica, where there was a slower pace of living. The island atmosphere was ripe for romance and decadence including Rastafarian music playing in the background.

The island greeting was hard to ignore. It was quite infectious when she began to listen with her heart and not with her head. Life was about taking risks and throwing caution to the wind, doing things to make your happiness more than just retirement living.

Her plane landed with a chorus of applause from those few in attendance. Hawaiian shirts and sunglasses came out to replace cold winter jackets and scarves. Coming from Chicago where winters could be harsh and cruel was depressing.

"I'm glad you talked me into this. Getting away from all of my worries sure does help a lot. I don't want to be anywhere where somebody is going to call my name. This is my chance to be invisible." Marta was a recent overseas transplant coming from the hot and humid climate in Saudi Arabia.

She had an adventurous spirit born to take life by the short hairs. Her father and mother taught her how to balance life and work without one overshadowing the other.

Her business was secretive when most believed she was a consummate salesperson. Money wasn't something she worried about when her bank account overflowed in abundance.

"The kids will be perfectly fine with your mother. We need this time to get back to what is really important in our lives. My work has kept me busy at the hospital. I barely see you when you come back from one escapade or another. I know traveling is part of your job but I was hoping this time we could do something together." Benjamin was thinking about his work, being wrist-deep in the blood of the innocent and the guilty.

He didn't make the distinction between the two when it was a matter of life and death.

Jamaica was bustling with activity with several people peddling their wares on the street corner, including weed.

Traffic was the survival of the fittest moving at a breakneck speed. Taxis were notorious for taking their lives and their passengers in the palm of their hands. It didn't seem to faze them how close to death they came every day.

Surrendering to the island moment was easy for most.

Marta was traveling with her husband Benjamin, an accomplished surgeon with a God complex. He didn't know the extent of her work. She was hired to find certain objects and people. The money was too hard to pass down when her research resulted in a reputation to precede her.

"I do my best to make time for my family. I don't get much downtime in my line of work, and neither do you. Unfortunately, we are both workaholics, unable to walk away from what we love. Jason and Jessica have learned to be independent when we're not around." Marta wasn't proud of some of the things she had done for the almighty dollar.

Benjamin was quite handsome with bleached teeth and newly acquired plugs to reclaim his youth. Being vain and sought after by the opposite sex had him playing fast and loose with his moral fiber. Sleeping with those who considered him their savior was hard to ignore when they were practically throwing it in his face. He was in his late forties, styling and profiling in a career that had his skills in demand.

His blond hair was out of a bottle, meant to hide the aging process that was sneaking up on him. He probably had a head of white and gray hair, but there was no way to know when he conscientiously dyed it every month without fail. He had a standing appointment with a vivacious and voluptuous stylist for more than a haircut.

"They're growing up so fast. I blinked and they became teenagers overnight. There's no getting that time back no matter how much I want to. Chantal raised them but we were there for every big milestone in their lives. Every recital and practice was recorded. One of us was always there no matter what our schedules were like." Benjamin thought about his last conquest, an aboriginal dynamo in the sack.

He was always drawn to short women with attitude. How he managed to nab Marta was beyond him. She was a long-legged statuesque Scandinavian beauty with the kind of body to stop traffic in the middle of rush hour.

They disembarked from the plane and made their way into the Airport. They had VIP status, making it possible to breeze through customs without much more than a dismissive wave. They still had to adhere to the rules. Money spoke volumes in countries where people lived by modest means.

"I'm never going to say we make the perfect parents. We did our best and they never wanted for anything. I'm glad to report both of them are going to college with their futures already written in stone. Jason is taking after you and Jessica wants to dip her toe into cooking. Going to culinary school will make her a well-rounded chef sought after by many," Marta said with pride in her heart.

There was no way she was going to mold her into her image. What she did was dangerous and navigating the pitfalls was like treading on thin ice. Benjamin thought this excursion was his idea. Marta had planted certain subliminal messages to nudge him in the right direction.

It was psychological warfare.

The people were friendly and courteous, not shoving and pushing like other airports.

They found their luggage with little effort and made their way to the front door with a blast of heat almost knocking Benjamin unconscious with one breath.

Marta felt like she was home in Jamaica. The benefit of traipsing around the globe following her father from one deployment to another was seeing the world from a different perspective. It brought back memories and she smiled even while the locals were staring at her in disbelief.

"Do you ever wish we could go back in time and do it all over again differently?" Benjamin questioned and began to contemplate the last fifteen years where they barely spoke one word to one another.

"There's no reason to have this debate here in paradise. We have two weeks of rest and relaxation to look forward to on a private beach in a private cabana. The drinks and food are paid for. It's not a resort, but simply off the map in uncharted territories. I got a great deal and I couldn't pass it up." She wheeled her fluorescent yellow suitcase behind her with one more expected at the villa when she arrived.

"I think we have made some mistakes and we should talk about them at some point during this vacation. Neither one of us is innocent. We need this time to reconnect. The passion in our relationship has fizzled. It's not like we have anything to be ashamed of. We agreed to have some fun on the side but never to talk about it. I would like to amend those arrangements." His fantasies revolved around Marta and another woman catering to his every sexual whim.

He had broached the topic with a few female colleagues with a variety of interests when they saw her photograph. He didn't know how easy it would be to have them licking their lips with a hunger to see her naked in the throes of ecstasy.

"It's all relative when you think about it. Pleasure comes in many forms. I've dabbled in a few things with your knowledge and permission. Black guys are my weakness. We are surrounded by healthy young men with an ebony persuasion. I wouldn't be opposed to grabbing one of them and showing you how wild I can be in the bedroom. The measuring stick is in their pants. I just don't want you to feel inferior when they bring the woman out of me too many times to count." She could see several specimens and her appetite for sex rivaled her business acumen.

"I'm not sure we are on the same page. What would you say, to being intimate with a woman when I'm in the room? What happens in Jamaica stays in Jamaica. I've always been fascinated by seeing you dominate another woman. To be told, I wouldn't mind seeing that dominant streak when I'm naked and at your mercy." He was putting it out there and felt there was no time like the present to learn new tricks under the cover of darkness.

"I've experimented with women in the past. It would be a first to do it with a man. I'm guessing you like the idea of being pleased orally by two women at the same time? To make it clear, I'm sure there are fantasies we can live out in the next two weeks. The island is full of adventure and excitement." She had this colorful sarong around her waist in this multicolor display of island culture.

Benjamin was rising to the occasion. There was no stopping the fantasies from coming to life in his mind's eye. Listening to the little head between his legs had gotten him into a lot of trouble in the past. Sneaking around and telling her half of what he had done was fun but doing it together would shed new light on the dynamic of their relationship.

Nobody was around to judge them unfairly. They could let their inner freak fly.

She shielded her face from the sun with her sunglasses taking the brunt of the glare.

There was a private car idling at the curb with a young man sporting a wide smile and open shirt with khaki pants.

"I do need some time to breathe. I lost count of how many surgeries I have done in the past week. There's always going to be somebody looking for my professional opinion. I have to remember life goes on without me. Somebody will pick up the slack in my absence." He took the liberty of grabbing her luggage and going to the back of the car to stow what they had brought with them, even though most of it was barely much more than floss.

The young man with a healthy amount of dreadlocks and muscular detail to his physique handed Marta a phone. It was discreet and subtle like some kind of handoff during an exchange between unsavory characters. They shared a knowing nod before he went and kept Benjamin distracted long enough for her to make the call.

She dialed the number and waited patiently to receive further instructions.

"I just landed. I'm guessing you are sending the rest of them before the end of the day. I hope you took my suggestions to heart. I want people I can trust to get the job done efficiently and with some expediency. Don't make me regret taking this on at the last minute." She said with the phone next to her ear.

"I hope this wasn't your idea of getting a fully paid vacation on my dime. You made your case abundantly clear with proof beyond a shadow of a doubt. We can't afford mistakes. They will be there after you have enjoyed the hospitality of the island. Getting there twenty-four hours before my soldiers affords you a window of opportunity." The man on the other side of the world was sitting with a Cuban cigar clutched between his fingers.

"I'm glad you see it my way. They came here on vacation but they're going to find more than they bargained for. Did they think they could hide from me? I just need a scent and I become a dog with a bone. I don't pretend to be the only one in this business. I'm the best and everybody knows it. It's not bragging when you can back it up with actions," She gloated with her hand multitasking looking at photographs of her prey unaware she was breathing down their neck.

Quinn Reynolds and Bryce Owens were going to rue the day they ever got on her radar. Betrayal and treason were two good reasons to personally oversee the mission. Ditching her husband was going to be easy with several young passionate women bought and paid for.

2

Two

It was a beautiful morning with the birds chirping and the sun dancing hotly on her skin. She was awake early at the crack of dawn, not about to lie back on her laurels even though the tropical setting was making her want to sleep in.

Training was in her blood.

Bryce was sound asleep in the room behind her with these white flimsy curtains billowing in the breeze. She stared off into space looking at the rolling waves crashing against the shore. This was her happy ending where she could finally let her guard down and be completely free with her libido.

The palm trees waved in greeting. A lizard slithered around her feet but she didn't jump out of her skin. Quinn had been around the world a few times without the chance to stop and smell the roses. A bullet with her enemy's name metaphorically stenciled on the surface was the only reason why she visited foreign lands.

She looked around. It was everything she wanted it to be. The place was beautiful and all they needed was a key code to get in when they arrived. An air bed and breakfast was all the rage spanning the globe to give owners the chance to find additional revenue by renting.

The only thing they needed was food, but there was a market nearby in walking distance. The fresh food and fruit was a daily pilgrimage. They had disposable income even though her funds had drastically been reduced.

Answers were far and in between, she had become frustrated with every dark alley turning into a dead end. She wanted to believe her brother was out there waiting for her to rescue him from a fate worse than death. Having that hope rekindled because of Bryce was a bitter pill to swallow. That fire to learn the truth was burning out of control. This was her one chance to decompress before continuing the search.

She still had injuries. They weren't skin deep. Mentally she was damaged beyond repair. Bryce was doing his best to curb her tendency to overreact to the slightest noise. Somehow she was able to sleep 5 hours without blinking into focus the darkness surrounding her from every angle. It took three days until she finally relaxed enough to close her eyes without the threat of reprisal invading her dreams.

"I'm guessing you have been up for quite some time." Bryce had shaved his head with only stubble remaining giving him a uniform crew cut from the military.

The beard was a nice touch to disguise him from possible identification.

"I was up earlier doing yoga and Krav Maga. I was going to wake you but you looked so peaceful. It's an ancient art and quite deadly when used correctly. I have several disciplines I have blended into one. It's time you learn how to defend yourself when there are no weapons within reach. The only thing you can count on is your own two hands." She thought about the several times she had gone toe to toe with the enemy when the gun was temporarily out of commission.

She didn't look like a soldier wearing her tiny little white bikini. Her flesh was bronzed and the buoyant shape of her breasts cut a swatch into the material with her nipples hard as stone.

"I get one day of reprieve before you mention beating the holy hell out of me. I thought I was doing better. Target practice has been this never-ending cycle of shooting one gun after another. I do admit I like the feeling of power in my hands." He held his hand out mimicking what he would do with a gun without any tremble of indecision.

"You seem to understand the basics. Don't fault me for wanting you to be ready for anything. Threats are not necessarily going to announce themselves when we are ready to answer. This place looks unassuming. I've already calculated three different egress routes out of here." There was the ocean but it was wide open when the easiest way was to use the cover of the trees to make a discreet exit.

Bryce was an analyst for an unscrupulous organization. He came looking for the hand of God to do his dirty work. Her name was synonymous with the mere mention of death. Learning more about her made him realize there was more to her than what could be seen skin deep.

The woman was wired tight with her senses on full alert twenty-four hours a day, seven days a week. The sex was phenomenal and it was the best he had ever had in his life. There was no comparison to the way she moved, like liquid fire over his body. Last night she was insatiable, with a four-hour marathon to leave him breathless in complete exhaustion.

"You must be rubbing off on me. I took the liberty of setting up some warning devices. They might be crude but they will do the job. It was easy to come up with designs with the Internet providing guidance and the blueprints. There's no way they can approach without us knowing a few steps ahead." He was still feeling the fatigue down to his bones, and his muscles burned from the exertion of her body driving him completely mad with desire.

"I hope I didn't hurt you last night. I can be rather rough when I get going. Those marks will fade in time," She said, referring to the scratches on his chest and back.

"A little bit of pain mixed in with pleasure can be a powerful aphrodisiac. I guess it's true what they say about hurting the ones you love. I like the idea of being on the same level. I rolled the dice and sometimes they came up snake eyes. I have no interest in going back to the way things were before we met." He had his hands on her shoulders massaging those tendons until they relaxed with a moan of compliance coming from her lips.

He did enjoy making her putty in his hand. It was the least he could you after putting her through the hell of thinking her brother was alive and well somewhere. The man responsible was still out there but he was reluctant to say the name out loud.

She didn't come home to a hero's welcome. Nobody knew what she did to protect the freedoms of others in several countries, some hard to pronounce.

It was a day in history shaping the political landscape and leadership of those countries demanding a change. She had the equalizer in the bullet when she had her scope on the target, dead set on making it their last breath on earth.

The gun with a powerful lens on the scope was sitting there by the barbecue. A couple of hours ago, she was taking fake shots at wild animals in the distance. It was her way of keeping fresh without the possibility of becoming complacent like some of her enemies when they thought there was no way anybody was going to get to them.

"I wish you could see yourself the way I see you. There is potential. I've seen soldiers ready to die for their country unable to pull the trigger. They lack a certain ingredient in the recipe. I've seen you face down your fears like a ferocious lion. Killing her still haunts me and I'm sure she is in your dreams." Her screams in the fire echoed in a way to wake them both up from a dead sleep in a cold sweat.

Bryce believed he was living somebody else's life. It wasn't his dreams he was worried about when his nightmares came calling. It didn't matter if they were in Paris or Rome. They were always surrounded by millions of people giving their enemies collateral damage. This way they were secluded away from the public.

Their new home was on the road without putting down permanent ties.

The thatch roof on their villa had seen better days. It was in desperate need of some repairs to prevent the elements from getting inside. They had gotten a deal on the promise they would do some required work around the place.

"I'm not built for the fight. I'm willing to undergo the training. I can't promise anything but maybe you can teach this dog some new tricks. I should get to work while there is daylight left. I'm not much for manual labor, but I don't mind rolling up my sleeves." He had learned certain things from the Internet including how to repair a thatch roof.

It was amazing what kind of research could be found when he went looking for it. Tutorials on anything were readily available at his fingertips. He was quite detail-oriented with an analytical mind. Following steps were easier than adapting or improvising.

The wooden ladder was already set up with a few repairs meeting with his approval. It was all about trial and error until he found the right mixture. Cutting down supplies was easy when he knew what to look for. Everything he needed was right there in the wilderness to secure the roof and make it livable.

"Tomorrow is when we see what you are made of. This vacation is going to be more than tropical drinks and lying in the sun. I want you ready. It's going to hurt more than you know. Getting up and doing it all over again will prove how strong you are. In the meantime, I'm going to get breakfast made for my hardworking man," She mocked with two fingers moving back and forth indicating it was the smallest violin playing just for him.

"Give me about an hour to follow these directions. I'm like a chef who doesn't just measure by guesswork. I'm very meticulous about everything I do. I don't see how training me is going to be any different than that. I've seen some teaching tools on the Internet about that mystical art you practice. I say this with the utmost respect but I wouldn't want to meet you in a dark alley alone." He climbed to the top and sat there looking at the ocean with its crystal blue persuasion beckoning him into the deep.

It was breathtaking. Perfect for framing in a postcard.

There was a crack of thunder. It was the twigs he had set up on the beach.

He saw a woman waving to him and they shared an awkward smile. Her blond hair was blowing in the breeze. The yellow bikini with white stripes down the side put her body on display.

Bryce squinted with his hand gripping the hammer like it was a phallic representation of what he was sporting inside his khaki pants.

"You must be my new neighbor. I thought I would come over and introduce myself. My name is Martha. I guess we will be seeing a lot of one another." With those words, she took off her bikini letting the shock absorb until he was staring unabashedly at her chest.

The bikini bottoms came off with a swift tug at the sides on either side. She had met the enemy and wasn't impressed. He didn't recognize the eyes of a soldier staring back at him. It was going to be like taking candy from a baby.

Behind a tree, a few yards away was a cachet of weapons loaded and ready for use. The soldiers would be there in a few hours and she was getting the lay of the land making her initial assessment before reporting back her findings.

She dove into the surf completely naked unencumbered by clothing. It felt good and refreshing. She knew without looking he was watching her every move. Her body was sculpted into a work of art. Admiring and praising her form was necessary when it came to the predictable actions of the opposite sex.

This was the calm before the storm.

3

Three

He waited patiently trying to determine the best approach when her anger was seething on the surface. Talking about Martha wasn't a good idea when Quinn showed her teeth of jealousy by chastising him for his behavior. It was a brief moment of temptation and it wasn't like he was going to do anything about a temporary condition to make his pants get a little tighter.

Quinn stood her ground showing no emotion almost able to predict what he was going to do next. This was going to be a lesson in humility he was never going to forget. Talking to 'her' was a mistake and staying secluded would keep them alive.

He had mistakenly thought she was jealous. That wasn't it. The seriousness of those coming after her was lost on him. She thought after the fire things would be different but he was still constantly letting down his guard.

"I don't have all day. Would you feel better if I put my hands behind my back like this?" She did exactly that including bending forward to give him a free shot. "What are you waiting for, an engraved invitation? I bet you think I'm going to make the first move. That's not how this works. You need to learn the enemy comes in every shape and size including a feminine form with an hourglass figure." She never moved an inch knowing from personal experience something was going to have to give.

"I didn't sleep with her. We had a conversation. It's not my fault she got naked and got my attention. I place the blame squarely on her. She's harmless.

I don't see any reason why we can't make friends. We should go over and make nice." He was angling for her to give in and see how foolish it was to always think somebody was after them.

She made a slight motion with two hands in a "come get some" childhood playground tactic.

She was more than the sum of every high and low in her life. She needed to know she could count on Bryce. Feeling something wasn't easy when she was numb from the waist down. There was no way she could afford either one of them to fall short resulting in their deaths.

He stepped forward with a swinging right cross. It was quick but unfortunately not quick enough. His identity was called into question when he landed unceremoniously at her feet looking up dazed and confused. He scrambled to his feet with his ego bruised in desperate need of inserting his physical dominance.

This time he tried going for a sweep but she easily leaped into the air like he had choreographed the move. A kick caught him on the jaw and he was spun in a circle in mid-air before coming back down at an awkward angle.

She knew he didn't belong in her world, where the worst of humanity could be found lurking in the shadows. His business behind the curtain was analytical with no real field experience. Getting him up to speed wasn't going to be easy when he was stubborn, still believing his weight advantage was his biggest strength.

"This is getting ridiculous. Do you really think I get any pleasure from hurting you like this?" She raised her finger and thumb to show that she found a bit of pleasure from making him her punching bag.

His anger was followed by the inevitable mistakes when he allowed his emotions to get the best of him. It was awkward and quite clumsy when he swung with grunts underneath his breath.

A roundhouse kick caught him on the temple and a sweeping blow to the back of his knees followed by her upper forearm smashing against his sternum brought him down onto the ground once again.

It was humiliating but there was no way he was going to give up until he got the upper hand. His embarrassment was meant to teach him a lesson. The only thing he could see was the way that she was mocking him with those expressionless features.

"I swear I'm going to wipe that smug look off of your face. Do you have any idea of how galling it is to be treated like a crash test dummy?" He charged and she moved a fraction of an inch to see him go flying over the picnic table on top of the deck.

"I could offer you a few tips. You are displaying your moves before you do them. It's all about instinct and sense memory. The more times you do something the better you are going to get at it. Let's try it again from the top. I will try to go easy on you but the only way you're going to learn is by fixing your mistakes," She advised still wearing a two-piece white bikini not conducive to hand to hand combat.

Quinn was mentally checking off a list in her head. She followed a strict adherence to the numbers knowing each move like the back of her hand. It was the way she was trained. She hated every moment but it gave her a thick skin. Life and death were serious business. Going through the humiliation of getting her ass handed to her was probably the best thing to ever happen to her.

"I don't need you to placate me." His ankle hurt more than the rest of his muscles but giving up wasn't something he was willing to do.

"I'm trying to prepare you. It seems you have forgotten what happened in the fire. If you had a polished portfolio in hand to hand combat that wouldn't have happened. Improvising is only going to get you so far in life. It works but there's also something called dumb luck. Something tells me you have never been in a real fight in your life." She was urging him on with subtle cues to infuriate him even further.

He stared at her with his left eye twitching and his upper lip quivering. His hands were shaking but then he learned to slow things down with a long calming breath. He breathed in and slowly exhaled the raw emotions trying to choke him to death.

She was taking him to task by showing him his weakness. Brute force was nothing without technique. Using an opponent's weight against them was the biggest weapon in her arsenal.

He was flipped into the air with her feet propelling him over her head. He screamed as he dropped eight feet to the ground below. He grunted and rolled down the incline slamming into a tree. It stopped his momentum and he was temporarily knocked unconscious unable to defend himself.

He could feel the sun against his eyelids and he blinked into focus to find Quinn standing over him with her hands on her hips.

"Are you through playing around? This is no time for a breather. Get up and come after me like a man. Maybe you should be the one wearing my panties." She purposely nudged his ribs to see him cringe in a way that pained her physically.

"You are having way too much fun at my expense. That fall could have killed me. Did that even enter into your thick skull? I'm not a mercenary for hire. My strengths are with my fingers on the keyboard of any computer. I know I have to change but you don't have to be a dick about it." He used the tree to climb to his shaky feet with a knot on the back of his head the size of a golf ball.

This time it was different. Taking the initiative wasn't going to work unless he had a plan of attack. He was through thinking he was going to hurt her. It was antiquated thinking when she had the obvious advantage with years of training under her belt.

Developing a technique would save him the heartache of looking up into his enemy's eyes pleading for mercy.

"I can do this all night. You're not going to stop until you have me on the ground." Her words conveyed it wasn't a bluff and she was prepared to hear him gripe all night long through squeals of pain until the lesson was learned.

He slammed his shoulder into her stomach lifting her clear off her feet. He had visions of bringing her down off of her lofty perch. It was an MMA maneuver he had seen on television. He wasn't expecting the slap to his ears to unbalance him.

He was in some kind of sleeper hold fighting for the right amount of oxygen into his lungs. His hands clawed at her forearms. Prying at her fingers only encouraged her to hum an old nursery rhyme underneath her breath.

She thought it was over and she was ready to mercilessly put his pain to an end. His arms went slack and his breathing was heavy indicating he was unconscious. When she let him go was when she got the surprise of her life.

His feet were firmly planted into the ground and she was knocked down when he pushed back with all of his weight behind it.

She saw stars when she was turned with the point of his knee in the small of her back. Struggling was pointless when he was using one of the moves she had taught him earlier in the night. It was impressive and she was ready to concede but not without a last-ditch effort to break free. His enemy was not going to show any kind of leniency which meant she couldn't let him think the tables had been turned.

A head butt and an elbow loosened his grip and she was able to break free moments before she passed out. She had him beat.

Bryce thought he finally went from the student to the master. It was too easy, and then it wasn't. He was calling uncle within seconds of having his shoulder almost taken out of its socket.

He stood to face her and saw the makings of a grin on the corners of her mouth.

"I think you need some time to recover. I wasn't expecting much but you have proven to be an avid pupil. There might be hope for you after all. I can see the reason why you think making friends is a good idea. I'm not of the same sentiment but I'm not going to stop you from getting to know our neighbor. Always keep your head on a swivel and don't take anything for granted. I'm going to bed." She took a few steps and then decided to play the same game as Martha.

The bikini top came off with her naked back exposed to his leering gaze. The bikini bottoms became a casualty of her two hands pulling at the strings similar to the way Martha had grabbed his undivided attention. Her golden globes hinted at the bright pink temptation beyond.

She was naked, feeling the freedom of having no clothes on with her raw sexuality driving her to look over her shoulder with the tip of her little finger in her mouth.

Bryce was a gasping with more than just the pain radiating through his limbs. It was guaranteed to be a night of sensuality and pleasures beyond his wildest dreams. He stumbled after her when they heard the unmistakable sound of tin cans rattling at the perimeter of their villa.

She ran naked to where a gun was strapped to one of the beams of the deck. It was unfortunate she didn't get a chance to use it before she was surrounded by men and one woman brandishing weapons.

"You are under arrest for high treason against the United States. It's in my authority to have you extradited back to the states." The man's voice was followed by his FBI credentials flashed in her face. They meant business.

Martha, AKA Marta was watching with a high powered pair of binoculars. This was a wrinkle she hadn't accounted for. This wasn't part of her plan. The timetable for the operation was no longer set in stone. She was going to have to adapt and stop them from taking her before they could get on a plane. Her men were waiting impatiently for their orders.

They were about to go on the hunt against their allies. It was tantamount to going to war.

4

Four

It was purely a coincidence, but then nothing was ever coincidental.

The room was silent except for a bit of mumbling from the other side of the room on the telephone.

Commander Evans was trying to confirm there was an exit strategy to bring Quinn to American justice. A mission under cloak and dagger had been revealed to be against the Geneva Convention. The details were quite explicit and her part wasn't for the faint of heart.

Quinn didn't like being in captivity and felt like a caged animal about ready to chew her arm off to get away. She wasn't foolish enough to make the mistake of fighting overwhelming odds. It was only going to end with her dead. The best thing to do was to wait and see how things were going to play out especially when Bryce was, unfortunately, the weak link.

They were restrained back to back in two chairs with this length of coarse fibered rope around their bodies, with metal chains secured to the floor to keep them from doing anything stupid. They struggled to test the resiliency to find there was very little give. They couldn't even move the chair, courtesy of how they had screwed the chain into the floor.

Quinn was able to verify what kind of weapons they were carrying. A few handheld revolvers were the only thing they would be able to smuggle in on short notice. It was possible they were working with black-market merchandise with the serial numbers scratched off.

Two women had her smiling wondering what their story was. The military was still primarily a man's world no matter what most people said to contradict it. Women still had to work their fingers to the bone to be noticed. These girls looked ready for a fight with their fingers twitching and licking their lips ready to pounce on anything that moved.

Commander Evans had twenty years of service under his belt. It didn't make him feel very good to go after one of their own but his orders were quite implicit. Quinn was considered a combatant despite her exemplary record. He had to believe they would sort it out in a tribunal to determine her guilt or innocence.

Their job was to get her in front of her accusers.

"It looks like our departure is being delayed because of inclement weather. Hurricane Flora is bearing down on the island with winds gusting to over 100 miles an hour. The island is locked down until further notice with no flights going in or out. It looks like you're stuck with us. I'm inclined to give you some rope in the hope you don't try to hang yourself with it." He knew her reputation for doing the impossible sometimes with the respect of her peers.

"The weather broadcast was unclear for the last few days. They were betting on the hurricane skimming the island but that was undetermined. It looks like they are going to get the brunt of it and we are smack dab in the middle of it. This isn't even close to how bad it's going to be. We need to fortify against the elements. You are going to need all the help you can get." Quinn could be very convincing and there was no explanation for why she was so damn good at her job.

"That's exactly what I was thinking. Just so we're clear on a few things. Somebody will be watching you at all times and you will have very little movement shackled together. Things haven't been going my way but I can improvise with the best of them. Against my better judgment, it will be easier to keep an eye on you without constantly worrying about your safety because of the hurricane," Commander Evans conceded on this issue and was still a little hesitant about giving her an inch afraid she was going to take a mile.

He had to admit the place wasn't up to building code. They had a lot of work to do before the hurricane arrived. It would take no prisoners and didn't discriminate over the elderly or youth. Everybody was fair game if they were caught with their pants down.

"I volunteer to look after them." Kendra had heard the stories about Quinn but didn't believe her legacy thinking it was exaggerated. "I'm younger than her and there's no way she is going to get the upper hand on me. Plus, I was the one who got the information on her whereabouts." She wanted the chance to show what she was made of with ice water running through her veins.

Most people could see from a first look that she was of Hawaiian descent. The dark hair with attitude to match and island blood made her a force to be reckoned with. She had been in several firefights with her boots on the ground soaked in the blood of her enemies. It was getting difficult to make the distinction when those lines had become blurred with their latest assignment.

"Be careful what you wish for, or you just might get it. By volunteering, you take full responsibility for anything that happens. We can all take turns and share the blame when those paying our salary come looking for answers. That is the worst-case scenario and I don't believe in taking any chances. Everything will be OK if we work together," He reassured, never one to lose the respect of his platoon when they were facing insurmountable odds.

"What about me? This has nothing to do with me. By your own admission, I'm not wanted and there is no warrant for my arrest. It seems unfair for you to treat me like a prisoner. I'm not guilty by association. We barely know one another. I've always told her the past has a funny way of catching up to her but she never listened," Bryce stated with some conviction in his voice.

The commander wasn't listening and was staring at the ominous black clouds rolling across the sky. It wasn't going to be good and finding shelter before the storm approached was going to take an amazing stroke of luck.

Their best bet was to hunker down and weather the storm.

Kendra and Francine had known each other for years. They met during basic training and struck up a friendship where they had each other's back. They worked amazingly well together with their body language speaking volumes over anything they could say with their mouths.

Those two girls took it upon themselves to attach the other side of the chain to their wrists. They had a duty to perform and they were not going to shy away from it. This would give them a chain gang mentality with them having weapons ready to be drawn at the slightest inclination of trouble.

Kendra and Francine were carbon copies of one another. Some had mistaken them for twins and others for sisters. They would do anything for one another with their loyalty to the flag and not necessarily to military conformity. They knew their prospects were limited and had ideas of padding their bank account for retirement.

"It appears you are one very popular lady. There is a bounty on your head for ten million dollars. You must have pissed in somebody's corn flakes to get them to issue that kind of monetary reward for your capture. I'm not concerned." He thought about the storm and smiled despite the danger.

"I see what you are getting at. A bounty isn't any good if they can't get to me. This storm has turned out to be a blessing in disguise for you. Nobody in their right mind would brave this weather for that kind of money," Quinn said sarcastically knowing full well there were some crazy sons of bitches willing to do anything for the almighty dollar.

The barometric pressure was dropping significantly with a change in temperature and wind velocity. It was the start. The full force of the storm was still miles away gaining speed and strength with the warm ocean to fuel it.

Nobody bothered to address Bryce and his squeaky voice in the din of military minds at work. He was forgotten, barely a nuisance better seen and not heard. They didn't take anything for granted and would watch him like a hawk tethered to Francine. It wasn't like he could fight back with any degree of success considering his amateur status.

The one thing they didn't know about him was his ability to improvise using his surroundings and environment to the best of his ability. He was already calculating certain odds and going through the analytics of several different scenarios in his head. It was all about the math and whether or not it added up to something he could live with.

"There's no time to debate. I've known people like you all of my life. I don't trust you. It's as simple as that. Thankfully, I don't have to trust you to work with you toward a common goal. Our safety is the main priority and we need to be on the same page to work together against Mother Nature at its worst."

He was betting on their need for self-preservation over running headlong into a storm that was plainly unpredictable.

"Commander Evans, we can have a temporary ceasefire until after the storm passes. My word is my bond and I suspect the same thing can be said for you. Let's not waste any more time bickering over silly little details like guilt or innocence. I can't read you into something that is classified and shouldn't have seen the light of day." Quinn was reminded of the mission and how their Intel was spotty at best.

Commander Evans and two of his unspoken platoon went outside to gather supplies and find something to board the windows up. The rental came with shutters which would need to be nailed down in case of hurricanes or other storms on the horizon. Those shutters were made of solid material built specifically to take a beating but nothing was for certain.

Quinn used whatever leverage she had to gather up all the canned goods. Electricity could go out at a moment's notice but it seemed their supplies would get them through a few days even with their visitors.

"*... has battered the surrounding islands with gale-force winds and over 200 plus millimeters of rain. Residents are warned to take every precaution. The storm is scheduled to stall over the island for the next twenty-four hours before slowly moving on losing steam in the ocean. There are sites set up and people are urged to evacuate to find a safe haven...*" The crackle of the radio was nothing compared to the way the branches were smacking against the windows getting louder and more frequent by the second.

Bryce made sure there was plenty of water in case their source became polluted. There were over 40 bottles in the fridge. Plenty of food was in the freezer section including steaks and ribs perfect for a barbecue. This was the only window of opportunity they were going to get for quite some time and they had to seize the day.

He was soon barbequing the meat and seasoning everything with a secret ingredient. It was risky with a recipe for disaster but he was going to need all the energy he could get and so were the soldiers. Canned goods could only go so far.

The pounding slowly extinguished the lights from outside where day had become night. Those shutters were shortly in place and ready for whatever was going to come their way. Nails secured them and there was an abundance of construction supplies under the deck in a small shed.

They had to break the lock but it was merely an obstacle to overcome.

The rain started a few minutes later and all three military personnel were soaked to the bone before they could finish their task. They came in looking like wet rats and smelling like them. Their clothes were sticking to them like a second skin and they decided to shed their black suits for something more conventional.

Khaki Camouflage was the color of choice. This made them feel superior even though it was a placebo effect. The enemy was fierce and they wouldn't be able to use the weapons they had brought with them to fight. Fear gripped them by the throats although they never showed it.

They were unaware of the spying eye of Marta from a few yards away using night vision goggles to watch their progress.

She made the signal and five men clad in black from head to toe were soon skulking down the beach with a silent approach. The guns strapped over their shoulders had silencers to keep their attack from being noticed until it was too late.

Marta could have easily walked into the fray leading the charge with whispered words of encouragement. She decided to be their eyes and ears. Watching with the night vision goggles and listening with a parabolic microphone was giving her an unfair advantage.

Technology was a bitch in the wrong hands.

Things were going to get ugly and there was going to be blood spilled before the end of the night. They had gone through every conceivable option in the last few hours. She was fully aware there were things left unaccounted for.

Plans had a tendency to go awry.

5

Five

It was early in the storm and there was nothing else they could do. Sitting idle and doing nothing wasn't their strong suit. They drank their water and fed their bellies with the food supplied on the barbecue before the storm started raging out of control.

"I have to give my compliments to the chef. It sticks in my craw how good these ribs are. I thought mine were the best but these are simply intoxicating and quite addictive. I would ask for the recipe if only the circumstances were better. I've almost forgotten there's a storm outside. You are the master of the barbecue and I bow down unworthy of tasting this kind of culinary genius." Commander Evans lifted one of the ribs and praised Bryce for a job well done.

"The secret ingredient is honey. It gives it that sweet flavor on the tip of your tongue. I don't like to brag. I do love how they turned out, especially since I was under the gun to finish them in time. I thrive on deadlines and pressure." Bryce wasn't just a nerd hiding underneath bulky clothing to prevent people from seeing his defined physique.

The girls in the platoon could see through his fake façade. Every ripple and involuntary flex of his muscles had their undivided attention. They both licked their lips with this insatiable thirst to guide him to the pleasure centers of their bodies.

They were subtle, unlike a man with a certain part of their anatomy rising to full salute in the presence of a feminine form. They were built to go the distance with the kind of stamina to leave their partner panting out of breath and exhausted after a marathon sex session with both of them.

"I don't like the way you are looking at him. He might not notice but I do. Men are oblivious. Sometimes you have to hit them over the head with a club to drag them back to your cave. I don't like to share my food and that sentiment goes for my man. He can look but he can never touch without my express permission." Quinn whispered into their ears while they were staring at Bryce undressing him with their eyes.

"I think I can speak for Francine when I say we don't mix business with pleasure. With that being said, I'm sure that temptation is hard to ignore for some and we're not going to tell you his magnetic personality isn't drawing us to him like a moth to a flame. You have no idea how lucky you are," Kendra sighed with visions of her last conquest thinking he was god's gift to women when he could barely cut the mustard in the bedroom.

She knew just looking at Bryce, there was a tiger underneath his compliance.

"He might look understated but I think we can both recognize a real man when we see one. I'm not going to admit what I already know to be the truth. I'm never going to spend the night alone again. He keeps me satisfied and forever young," Quinn praised without an ounce of shame for treating him like a piece of meat.

"It's been quite some time since I have been satisfied in that way. I think I might have to find a man worthy of my skills in the bedroom. It's not as easy as it sounds. I wouldn't even dream of testing the chemistry with these guys. We have to be on the same level to work together with some efficiency. I just want that one toe-curling orgasm." Francine didn't know why she was sharing but it did feel good to release some of that pent-up sexual aggression with her words.

A branch broke free from the tree outside the window. It smashed into the shutters. The room fell silent when that window exploded inward. Nobody was near enough to feel the shards of glass cutting into their skin. It did make them jump back when those shutters buckled underneath the weight of the impact. It stayed intact, but for how long was anybody's guess.

Commander Evans raced with his two comrades in arms to barricade the window in case of a breach. It wasn't going to end like that. Nothing lasted forever and the storm was no different. It was stalled over the island like the weatherman had predicted and was soon lashing the shore with rain and wind accompanying it.

It was dark outside at 7:00 PM.

Dinner was no longer a much-needed distraction.

Their nerves were frayed and they had frazzled expressions on their faces. This was not what they were trained for. There were storms similar to these during several of their missions overseas in foreign countries where they shouldn't have been spotted.

High-level targets were marked for assassination.

"We both know we should leave here and find better shelter. The roads are probably impassable with downed trees and power lines. It looks like we are stuck with one another until this is over. I think it's fair to warn you I haven't begun to fight," Quinn warned having a bit of fun at his expense to keep them guessing about what she was thinking.

"I do love a challenge. I know not everything is as it seems. I'm no stranger to being part of a mission where the parameters are sketchy at best. I wish it could be different." He turned when the doors to the deck began to rattle on their hinges.

The wind was howling attempting to get in.

"It's not necessary for us to be at each other's throats. You don't know the full story and nobody should. I was there but I was merely a spectator for the most part. Innocent civilians died and I carry that burden every day of my life. It could have been avoided but there's no way to go back and change things. If there was, I would do it in a heartbeat without even thinking about it. I was naïve to think that my superiors had all the answers when they didn't even know the questions," She explained in terms he could understand and the knowing nod made her realize this was something he had come across in his 20 years.

He got up and paced back and forth, waiting for the next calamity to fall at his feet. He didn't have to wait long when part of the roof came off. Their shelter was being taken apart one piece at a time and soon they were going to become a casualty of a war against Mother Nature.

The rain was coming down in sheets and they had to move to the other side of the villa waiting out the storm that had barely begun.

"If this keeps up, we're going to have to leave and risk injury in the storm. We have the force to break down a door and storm the castle. Kendra noticed an estate up the road guarded by a black wrought iron gate. We can easily bypass their security and get inside. I didn't see any vacancy signs but we can make our own. This only works if we have a unanimous vote." Commander Evans would contend with the inhabitants but the owners could've sought out shelter somewhere else instead of braving the storm.

It was also possible nobody was there.

"This place isn't going to hold up for much longer. I did my best to repair the roof but I'm no carpenter. It's not fit for man nor beast outside. You have my vote." Bryce didn't want to be there when the whole thing came crumbling down around their ears.

There was a consensus. All of them were willing to risk certain injury by walking out of the only shelter they had. It was flimsy and was tearing apart with only the shutters keeping the elements from getting inside.

"I don't want to be the one to say this but there's something we haven't thought about. We have been selfishly thinking about ourselves when others might be in the same boat. We have a new neighbor down the beach we should look in on. It's not part of your mandate but I don't see why we can't make the effort." Quinn was showing her compassion even with the chain around her wrist chafing.

Commander Evans understood sacrifice. These were not actions of a guilty person and he was starting to reconsider his orders. Being in the wrong place at the wrong time shouldn't have been a convictable offense. He needed more information before making an educated decision.

She wasn't willing to reveal any more information regarding the reason why she was being accused of treason. What could have possibly happened to make them disallow any knowledge of her actions?

She was the scapegoat to keep others from having their head on the chopping block. It was a scenario old as time where those in higher positions of power couldn't be trusted to do the right thing by coming clean. They would rather make somebody else pay for their crimes.

They gathered up whatever supplies they could carry.

Seven people were about to embark on a new adventure of danger and excitement. Three of them went ahead to secure the new location while Commander Evans took the liberty of taking Quinn's advice about making sure others were safe before they would follow.

"I don't know how you talked me into this. My training isn't up for debate. I hate to admit when I'm wrong, but you're right. I'm no better than the pencil pushers in Washington if I stand idly by and do nothing. Don't make me regret this. We have Bryce as collateral if you decide to run. I will make sure to throw the book at him for aiding and abetting a criminal," He threatened but it was an idle threat considering a good lawyer could get Bryce off with a slap on the wrist.

"The only thing I'm worried about is what Francine and Kendra are going to do with Bryce in my absence. You can't tell me you haven't noticed the way they have been looking at him. I wouldn't be surprised to walk in to find him naked and tied up to the bed with them abusing his body for their own sexual amusement." She could see the storm raging but it was nothing compared to losing the man she was destined to spend the rest of her life with.

"They are professionals and will act accordingly. They know the score. This is a mission and not some holiday. We have to keep on task without any distractions to get in the way. I like you more than I'm willing to admit. I think under different circumstances we could've been friends or maybe even colleagues, fighting on the same side. We are more similar than you realize." He packed a bag and looked over at the unspoken duo with very little to say.

They were not standing at attention.

Their backs were turned and they were sitting on the couch in front of the window. It appeared they were sleeping with their chins touching their chest. It gave him a queasy feeling in his gizzard he couldn't shake.

Two holes punctured the shutters.

"Are you listening to me? I'm trying to tell you something personal and you're not even paying attention." Quinn grabbed his shoulder only to have her fingers shrugged free with him walking toward his two platoon members.

He raised his finger for silence. The scene was set and the tone was easily recognizable from other times where he had been betrayed. Death followed him as his own personal shadow and this was no different. He didn't want to believe it was happening again. The proof was seeing it up close and personal.

He gulped when he stood in front of them looking at the two precise holes in the center of their foreheads. They were dead and he didn't hear a thing ,which meant somebody was out in the storm playing a game of cat and mouse.

6

Six

It was a moment captured in time where nothing made any sense. The bounty was out there and to think nobody was going to take advantage of it was completely insane. He was wrong to believe the island was a safe haven. The storm wouldn't stop somebody from coming after their prize. Especially when the money was in the millions.

He thought about the bounty and what lengths somebody was willing to go to. It was obvious when he began thinking about it without the cloud of his orders getting in the way.

Quinn was innocent and somebody was using her past to put her in the crosshairs of several people vying for the money at the end of a bullet.

They both dived for cover when the room suddenly became a shooting gallery. The bullets cut through everything in their path turning the villa from a paradise into a nightmare. Whoever was out there was driving the nail into their coffin one bullet at a time.

"I don't know about you but I'm getting tired of being three steps behind. Give me room to maneuver without the restriction of these chains around my wrist. I know I'm asking a lot. You're going to need all the help you can get if you want to make it out of this alive. I estimate five guys by the angle of the bullets. It's a good guess and I think you already know that." Quinn was behind the couch, the stuffing flying everywhere making a snowstorm inside the villa.

"I shouldn't do this. This is only asking for trouble. I can't do this alone." He reached out and offered the key to her freedom which she eagerly accepted.

"I promise I'm not going to run and leave you stranded in a fight you can't win. We are in this together until the bitter end. You don't know how much I can help you. This bounty is literally going to be the death of me. I've already had people come after me for personal reasons. This is strictly about the money. My friends can become enemies for a price. We are going to have to split up." She received a nod of confirmation.

"I agree with your assessment. It makes complete sense but I don't like being unable to see you. I'm still going to take you in. I have no choice. Let's do this. Give them hell and make them wish they never came after you." He knew it wasn't a good idea for a frontal assault however keeping them occupied would give Quinn a better chance to use the element of surprise against them.

To this end, he came out of hiding long enough to fire several shots without any real pattern. It was meant to put them on the offensive and to make them believe his arsenal was unlimited. He was down to his final few bullets and he was going to keep them until the last possible second when he saw the whites of their eyes.

He crawled across the floor, avoiding the shards of glass that had blown in courtesy of the storm. The roof was barely hanging in there. They had something else to worry about besides Mother Nature's wrath. She was a formidable bitch blowing with enough force to lift the villa from its foundation.

The only thing keeping it grounded was the deck attached to it with its beams securely driven into the ground. Without it, the villa would've been destroyed beyond recognition. It was still shaking threatening to tear apart at the seams but somehow it weathered the worst of the storm before the eye was overhead.

These were not the dark ages and technology had come a long way.

Trying to hold in the scream of defiance was making him bite his tongue waiting for the right time to strike. He had all that he could handle with them advancing, the sound of their footsteps pounding in his head.

Quinn watched his lone wolf routine and smiled thinking he was one of the good ones. It didn't make sense to admire the man when he was going to bring her in by any means necessary. It was his job and she couldn't fault him for following orders even if it was blindly.

There was no back door. Mother Nature had taken care of that. A hole big enough to slide through put her in the thick of things. The rain was more of a drizzle but the wind almost knocked her off of her feet. She had to hold onto something for support and used the trees bending to the dominance of the wind.

She wasn't able to see much until her eyes adjusted to the darkness. It was a gift which afforded her a better chance of seeing her enemies before they saw her. She would much rather be in bed sleeping because life was easier in dreams than reality.

Shaking her head gave her a chance to think about the best approach.

A man appeared wearing a black rain slicker. He was moving slowly with his rifle outstretched and finger on the trigger ready to mow down anything in his path.

He was well aware of what he was up against and thought he was prepared. The mission had changed with the parameters becoming more of a capture than a kill. The money made him hungry and he could think of many things he could do with his share of the bounty. He could see the sports car with a huge house on the beach someplace tropical calling his name.

The hand over his mouth came out of nowhere, with an arm across his throat cutting off his windpipe. He tried to lift his gun but it was summarily slapped out of his hands with something hard enough to make his fingers tingle.

"I don't want to kill you. Just relax and take your medicine like a big boy. Falling asleep isn't the worst thing that can happen to you. You'll wake up with a headache but it's better than the alternative in a box that is 6 feet under." Quinn applied more pressure while listening to his breathing get faster until he was gasping.

The gun he was carrying was hanging loosely over his shoulder with his hand trying in vain to break her grip.

She would have killed him had it been a combatant. Her initial assessment confirmed he was American. Being paid to do a job was something she could respect. The money was hard for anybody to ignore no matter their skill level or military training. He carried himself like someone who had been there and done that too many times to count.

It felt like an eternity but finally, he slumped heavily into her arms. She continued for a few beats more. She was careful not to kill him. Dropping him into the brush underneath the canopy of some trees would protect him from the elements.

Quinn searched his body and found several different things, including a radio. It would be good to have some forewarned knowledge. She didn't even have to bother turning it to the right frequency when it was already there.

"*I don't see her. Somebody report in and tell me you have things under control. We all know the price for failure. I have it on good authority our employer isn't going to tolerate anything less than success.*" The female voice was with a tone indicative of a general leading the charge into battle.

"*We are about to go in. There was some resistance. It's been pretty quiet for the past couple of minutes. I would hazard to guess they're waiting to use the rest of their ammunition. I'm not getting any answer from Reggie. It's probably just because of the storm.*" The radio crackled in her hand and she turned down the volume before finding the attached ear bud so she could listen in without anybody being the wiser.

She had to return to the house. It was tempting to walk away. The easiest thing to do was to find Bryce and get him out of hot water before they made tracks. Her promise was her bond and leaving would make her sick to her stomach.

A shadow loomed over her, the metal bar she had used to disarm Reggie wasn't going to make a dent in the hulking figure standing in front of her. He was a mountain of a man dwarfing her and making her feel inferior, which was the point of the exercise.

"It's not nice to eavesdrop on a private conversation. I heard the radio. You must be daft to think a bloke like me wouldn't know what you were up to. You can take your chances by going toe to toe with me but I wouldn't advise it. Give up and maybe I won't have to hurt you, unnecessarily damaging the merchandise. They want you alive but they didn't say in how many pieces. Breaking your arm and a couple of ribs will make you less of a threat." Landon was British, recently transplanted to the states to become a member of an elite squad with a lucrative contract under his belt.

His beard was dripping with water and his eyes were staring right through her.

"If it's all the same to you, I think I'm going to take my chances. It might surprise you to learn I've taken down bigger opponents than you. It's all about using your weight against you. A lumbering idiot is a detriment to his men when brute force isn't any better than a gorilla pounding his chest. You might be a beast amongst little boys but I'm not afraid of you." She said the words while she stared daggers of defiance in his direction.

"This is going to be the most fun I've had in quite some time. I like your confidence. What you're looking at is a prized stallion with not an ounce of fat. This is all muscle and quite formidable against any opponent. I'm not a lumbering idiot. I think before I act. It's certifiable for me to see you as a viable threat." He almost laughed when he began choking from the impact of a knife-edge chop to his throat.

She jumped on top of him with the palms of her hands slapping at his ears to screw up his balance. He stumbled when he received a head butt. Quinn was using everything she could think of including gouging at his eyes to get the upper hand.

He was using his hands to deflect as much of the attack as he could. Flailing his limbs and fighting for some kind of offense wasn't easy when she was continually pummeling him without mercy.

Quinn was on his back driving her elbows into his shoulders and the back of his neck. She was relentless with a tenacious attitude to make any enemy reconsider their options.

"You speak a good game but I have yet to see you back it up with actions. I'm just a frail little woman and you are a big bad man. You can't possibly believe any of that in this day and age." She taunted, as she dropped down behind him using her foot to feel the pleasant crack of his knee, dropping him to the ground in a compromising position.

"That will be enough of that," A voice commanded. It was the same one she heard on the radio.

The click of the gun made her cease the attack with her arms in the air.

7

Seven

Bryce didn't feel very good about breaking and entering, but then again, he had done some questionable things over the last few months. It was distasteful to see these girls working in unison, not the least bit concerned about the consequences.

"I would say the lights are out and nobody is home. The whole block is in darkness. The grid for this area is probably down. There are no cars in the driveway. The evidence suggests the place is vacant. It's built of solid brick and those shutters are made of steel. These people knew what they were doing when they built on a tropical island prone to hurricanes and other storms." Kendra was fiddling with the lock, after already cutting the security cable thinking it might be on a different frequency.

"I want to go on the record to say that this is a bad idea. I know it's better to ask for forgiveness than permission in this instance." He received a saucy little smile in return.

"I'm going to remind you of what you just said later tonight." Francine was already envisioning moments of unrestrained passion under the sheets.

"Leave the man alone. You have a very high sex drive. I didn't want to say anything before but it does get you into trouble. Do I need to remind you what happened in Switzerland?" Kendra was kneeling in a position to see the bulge of his arousal right in front of her eyes.

It was temporarily distracting but she was able to multitask with the best of them. She had her ear to the grindstone listening for any unusual sounds inside. There was nothing. The silence was comforting in a strange and unusual way. She knew the eye of the storm was passing and they would once again be bombarded by wind and rain, the likes of which she hadn't seen since she was in India during a tsunami.

Bryce was nervous to feel their eyes on him. Usually, he was pretty oblivious to their interest but civilian females had nothing on these military figures of persuasion.

He wasn't prone to water cooler gossip. He never made assumptions until he got to know somebody. This was a little different with them protecting him while at the same time making him feel uncomfortable.

There was a crack as a tree came down directly behind them, less than a couple of feet away. Two more followed like dominoes blocking the driveway and the road beyond.

It would be a huge undertaking to clean up the mess after the storm had passed.

"I would suggest getting inside where it's safe. I'm not sure if you've noticed, but there are plenty of other trees ready to come down. We can't trust luck. Sooner or later another one is going to come down and we're going to be under it," Bryce muttered under his breath trying to convey the seriousness of the situation without panicking.

"If you think you can do any better then, by all means, take over from where I left off. Everybody's a critic. I'm going around back to see if there's another way in." Kendra was exasperated and didn't feel like having her work under a microscope with both of them looking over her shoulder.

She disappeared around the corner shrouded in the shadows.

"I thought she was never going to leave. I don't mind telling you how delicious you look. I might be of the minority but I like civilians with that little trace of fear in their eyes. She's a little too subtle but I like the forward approach better than waiting for something to happen." She pushed him up against the door and began tracing his muscles with her fingertips avoiding the one dancing a different tune inside his pants.

"I can't say I mind the attention but this is wrong. I know it doesn't seem like it from your vantage point. The excitement is setting you off and giving you that adrenaline rush. It's not me. It could be anybody and you would still be all over them like a cheap suit." He was trying to discreetly let her down without causing her to feel it was a rejection.

She growled with her fingers pressing into his chest to scratch at his nipples underneath the fabric. It was fun to treat a man with careless disregard. She was getting a kick out of seeing him squirm with his hands at his side. Licking her lips had her staring at the object of her fascination with hungry pursuit.

There was no way for Bryce to censor his words when he was up against a woman with one thing on her mind. The soldier had been replaced with a woman on the prowl with an insatiable need he could help her with. It was interesting to see her let her hair down. It was true about men and women.

Women thought about sex as much as men but they were unwilling to admit it. It was a known fact hidden from public scrutiny. Cheating was a two-way street. Women hit their sexual peak when they were over 40 and men hit theirs in their teens and early twenties.

A lonely woman in the prime of her life would seek out a younger representation of what they were getting at home. Older women could entice and seduce with very little effort. Experience came with wisdom to bring those boys into their yard looking to learn a few life lessons under the sheets.

"I know you're not going to like hearing this but this isn't going to happen. It's not anything to do with you. If I were any other man, I would gladly take you up on your offer for some much-needed relief. I have needs like everybody else. I love her. There, I said the words...are you happy? I have been locked up in these chains for too long." The only way he was going to change his life was to admit what he was denying and open up his heart to love.

It wasn't fair to feel this way inside. She was the one who could make him turn around and say those three little words on the tip of his tongue. He just had to hold on for a few more hours until he was able to say them to the woman who had become very important to him.

"Are you really comfortable doing nothing about this heat between us? Nobody can blame you for your unhappiness when you have gotten yourself into this situation. This is your chance to let your worries pass you by."

Francine had been there before and wasn't above using psychological warfare to make him change his mind.

"I know there's pain in your eyes. Somebody hurt you and you have been trying to forget them by jumping anything with two legs. There's no reason to deny it. I can see it written on your face. Do yourself a favor and let yourself heal before you jump into anything." He was playing armchair psychiatrist by delving deeper into her psyche without much to go on other than her body language.

"Way to ruin the mood. I was running hot but now I'm ice cold. For your information, I'm good at keeping my distance but I hate to admit how he makes me feel. The sex is too good and we both know the only thing we are good for is a few hours of carnal delight. I want something better than to go down the same path over and over again." It felt good to say the words.

The door swung open with a long drawn out creak which was a little deafening to their ears.

Bryce was listening to his heart when everything meant nothing when he wasn't with her. It was a messy affair taken right out of the pages of a tabloid magazine. How he met her by recruiting her services under false pretenses could've been a storyline in any daytime serial.

A flashlight led the way and the place was immaculate. The gray hardwood floors were accented by black metal grates over the vents. The architecture was suburban with a trace of industrial. A farm sink could easily be seen from where they were standing in a wide-open design.

There was ambient heat coming from the floorboards under their feet.

They both looked at each other, becoming aware the house was on some kind of generator. The lights came on instinctively. It was their movement that activated the controls, including a blazing fire in the fireplace accompanied by a bearskin rug.

"That is the dictionary meaning of romance right there. I can help you let go and you don't have to be alone tonight. It doesn't mean we have to have sex. I could just hold you," Bryce wondered out loud how he was going to stop her from taking advantage of the situation.

"That's sweet and sounds delightful. It won't cure the itch I can't scratch alone. There is no shortage of men willing to give me what I want. You ruined your chances by opening up your mouth. There are many ways to appear ugly and it doesn't have to do with your appearance." Francine flashed the beam around the room to see black leather furniture and a huge 65-inch television adorning the wall over the fireplace.

There was no expense spared in the construction and décor of the place. It didn't remind Bryce of being in the tropics. There were no splashes of color with every room painted in a neutral tone.

The expanse of the beach could be seen courtesy of electric lit torches on the path leading to the white-hot sand. The pressure treated wood of the deck would keep the elements at bay. The salt air was like cancer to any wood surface. The brick façade cost a pretty penny but would weather the elements over the course of several years without degradation.

"I love the smell of cinnamon." Francine lit a candle and stood there inhaling the fragrance with her eyes closed.

The storm was outside raging and they couldn't hear a thing. The walls muted the storm giving them a moment to breathe without thinking the walls were going to come down.

"I'm glad you're having a good time but maybe we can concentrate on checking out the house before you get too comfortable. We still don't know if we are alone. I would hate to disturb somebody's peaceful slumber and make them act irrationally when they feel threatened." Bryce advised.

Bryce knew that he was trying to fill some kind of void in his life and needed more than words to convince him it was a good idea to commit to a long-term relationship.

"Give me a minute. This takes me back to a different time and place in my life when things were simple. I sometimes wonder if I made the right decision by going into the military with my eyes wide open. I did have a different path in mind. Don't laugh. I was thinking I could be a veterinarian. It sounds absurd when I say it out loud." Francine put down the gun and used the flashlight to see a family tree of young privileged children growing up in the lap of luxury.

"We are invading someone's personal space. I don't like this and I'm getting a very bad feeling in my stomach. I've learned to trust those gut instincts. We should clear the other rooms. Where is Kendra? I thought she was looking for another way in. It seems rather unusual for a woman of her skill set to be missing in action without a good reason," He said not realizing what had come out of his mouth was a mouthful.

Somebody cleared their throat and there was the cock of a shotgun.

They turned slowly to see a disheveled man in a silk red robe with a crop of blond hair standing in front of Kendra with a shotgun pressed into her spine.

8

Eight

The storm had picked up in force and velocity.

The chair shook underneath her feet and somehow she had managed to jump out of the frying pan and into the fire. Everybody was looking for her and nobody was willing to share which meant there was a war being fought on two different sides.

"Tell me again how one woman was able to disarm you. I thought you were the best money could buy. Those testimonials on your security website are lying. You let a woman without a weapon bring down two of you. I would count yourselves lucky you are still breathing, considering her background. You took her lightly and she made you pay for it. What about the other one?" She asked with her mind going a million miles an hour trying to figure out what to do next.

"There was nobody there. We searched the area quite extensively until we had to call it off due to the weather. The place was destroyed and was leveled by the storm. Nobody could have survived something like that. The person with her must've been buried underneath the rubble. I doubt we'll be seeing anything more of him. At least that is one headache we don't have to worry about." The soldier had decided to play it safe by giving her nothing but the facts.

"What you say would have more conviction had I not found you unconscious at her feet. I'm beginning to think your company's reputation was built on a pack of lies. It's a house of cards. I won't be using their services again. It's not what you have done for me in the past but what have you done for me lately that matters," She related, and was quite adamant about cutting the cord even after a lucrative partnership for the past five years.

"She's a pit bull. I couldn't get her off of me. That girl is a wild animal. I make no apologies or excuses for what happened. I thought the stories about her were embellished. They say she broke down some glass ceiling for women in this profession. I remember the day when men made the rules and everybody else followed them." Brandon was speaking before he realized it was better to know his audience before saying anything to ruffle their feathers.

"That is a sexist thing to say to me. Get out of my sight. Go and relieve Eric. I have a good mind to blacklist you. It would serve you right to be standing in the unemployment line waiting for whatever meager check they put in your hand. I'm dealing with morons who think women are inferior to them. I think you know the truth." She threw up her hands and turned her back, the sound of his footsteps receding until the door closed.

"Good help is hard to find these days. I know you don't believe in women's equality. Do you think you would have had this problem with a strictly female platoon of soldiers? I think you already know the answer. I commend you on being at the head of the spear. I would applaud you but my hands are presently tied behind my back." Quinn tried to move with the knots getting tighter almost cutting off the circulation to her fingers.

"You understand nothing about me. Don't even think about trying to get in my good graces. I have a one-track mind when it comes to business. It's all about the money. I had everything set up until another player stepped onto the chessboard. We are getting you off this island tonight. I can't be certain, but I got the feeling from the phone call the person looking to take you alive is here on the island." That one call was a little disturbing and had her reconsidering her career options.

"That's good to know. I feel there's a puppet master behind all of this and it's not who I thought it was. I've been running around in circles fighting my shadow. Somebody is going to great lengths to keep me preoccupied. They have gone digging into graves that should never be unearthed. I look back at the past with trepidation and regret." Quinn had done some bad things for good reasons but she should have realized there was an equal and opposite reaction.

"Cry me a river. We all have problems. The logistics of getting you off the island before the storm passes isn't very good. I could call in a favor but it's going to cost me some credibility. My employer is steadfast about remaining anonymous. I don't want to put him on the spot unless absolutely necessary. You are quick on your feet and maybe you can help me. It would benefit us both to get off the island before gun-toting maniacs come looking for you." Marta was looking for an alternative route and was depending on her prisoner to offer up some suggestions.

There was an empty space in the shadow beside Quinn. She could hear his distant voice and tuning him out was impossible. It was uncanny how he could say the right thing at the right time to make her feel better. He was able to finally crack the code to her happiness which included having his arms wrapped around her.

"Let me get this straight so there is no misunderstanding. You want me to help you. It's a little funny when you think about it, but it does make some sense. I don't want to be hunted for a trophy. The bounty makes this island susceptible to all sorts of unsavory characters looking to capitalize on it. This is an untouched paradise with a legacy and heritage that goes back centuries." The responsibility of the indigenous people was weighing heavily on her shoulders.

"Whatever makes you sleep better at night is fine by me. I have been told by several different sources there's no way off of the island during the storm. Money has power in the right hands. My employer has deep pockets. All I have to do is ask for a little off the top of the bounty." Marta tugged at the handcuffs making sure they were secure with no wiggle room for error.

The smell of jasmine and lavender assaulted her senses. It was a brilliant combination to tantalize her olfactory sense. She felt lucky the bounty explicitly instructed she had to be taken alive. There was a codicil in the contract stating her death would result in half of the bounty.

Five million was more than enough for some people to take the shot from a distance in order to prevent getting their hands dirty. Too many things could go wrong during an extraction when shooting a prey dead would be preferable.

It was 4:00 AM and the storm was expected to continue into the late afternoon before conditions improved. The cleanup would extend into weeks and even months with millions reported in damages. Those displaced from their homes would come back to a sight worth more than a thousand words.

"Hypothetically, being on the lam would make it necessary to cultivate some sources on the island. Contrary to popular opinion, I can be very persuasive with more than a gun in your face. There might or might not be a boat fueled and ready to go when they get my phone call. I could, hypothetically, let you in on the little secret but I don't see what is in it for me," Quinn hinted at some kind of beneficial and mutually exclusive arrangement between the two of them.

"What are you suggesting? Take into account I'm not going to give up my bounty. That money is going to be in my hands before the end of the day. That's not conjecture. That's a spoiler." Marta already had plans for the money and it didn't involve cutting her in on the action.

Quinn motioned for her to come closer and she whispered what she wanted keeping it short and concise. They separated and stared at each other without another word spoken for at least one full minute.

"You are a crafty one and maybe I did underestimate you. That is not going to happen again. I don't make the same mistake twice. I learn from them and move on. What you are suggesting can be done in theory. It goes against everything I believe in. I'm willing to entertain this idea but only if you have something important to contribute." Marta was purposely beating her into revealing her secret stowed away boat fueled and ready to go at a moment's notice.

"I'm glad, and I'm going to take it on face value you can be reasoned with. As a gesture of good faith, I'm going to give you the phone number to call but not the code to release the boat into your care. I will need something in writing and notarized. Call it covering my bases. I don't think you would do anything less." They came from similar backgrounds built from the same cloth of defiance.

The storm was the stumbling block and clearing a path to where the boat was located wasn't going to be child's play.

Marta dialed the number and waited to confirm there was a boat.

"They want to talk to you before releasing any of the information. I admit this is very impressive and I could use somebody with your skills on my team. Let that sink into your skull and maybe we can talk about a different kind of future for you." Marta loved to have people she could trust in her inner circle and was willing to make some concessions to have somebody like Quinn doing what she did best.

Quinn talked to the old man on the phone and then handed the receiver back to Marta.

There was a boat fueled a few miles away in a non-disclosed location.

"You have given me a lot to think about and I will take it all under advisement. We seem to have reached an agreement. There are still a few things to iron out. I'm expecting a quid pro quo. I was courteous enough to give you a gesture of good faith and it would be a good idea for you to return the favor." Quinn dangled the chains and was soon unleashed to the chagrin of her captor.

"I don't know how I can trust you. You have a track record of betraying anybody you work with. I should have my head examined for even entertaining this idea. This is a one time offer not to be repeated. There is a clock on your answer and it begins ticking right now." Marta began moving her finger back and forth making the motion of a ticking metronome.

Her phone began ringing and she picked it up. She turned her back and had a private conversation before turning with a huge smile on her face.

"It appears the report of your colleague's death was premature. My employer has informed me he has your friend and his two protectors. This is where we change the fine print in the contract. You're going to take me to this boat and we're going to meet up with your friend and the two girls he was with. Do anything else and they will die horribly in ways you can only imagine. That's what you call leverage," She said smugly before restraining her to the chair once again in a position of power.

9

Nine

The water was choppy with the waves peaking at ten feet tall, courtesy of the hurricane turning the sea into a death trap. There was no sense in arguing with the mighty force of the storm when there was no way to reason with it.

The dock was vacant with not a living soul in the vicinity except, for some brave and somewhat idiotic men and women out to conduct a negotiation. The van was rocking back and forth with the springs being tested by the way the hurricane was taking exception to them being out when everybody else was hunkered inside.

"We just have to wait for the right time and we will be on our way. The exchange is pretty simple. You leave with me and I provide proof of life when we are far enough away from shore. My benefactor should be here shortly. The arrangements are already made." Marta was surrounded by burly men with no expressions and their loyalty bought with more money than they were going to be able to spend in a lifetime.

"I'm not going to do anything foolish. His life means more to me than my own. I hear the words but they sound foreign coming from my mouth." Quinn shook her head with her breath short thinking about the possibility of never seeing him again.

"Isn't it funny how plans never go the way you want them to? I thought I accounted for everything. This storm was only a whisper of a problem. I thought the odds of it striking the island were slim to none. I should never assume anything in this line of work. Bryce could be coming with us. I wouldn't mind the company. Unfortunately, the women are of no use to me and will have to be neutralized," Marta offered an alternative to keep the two lovers together until the end.

"I'm reminded of an old saying. If you love someone set them free. I can't in good conscience bring him along for the ride. It would be selfish. As much as it pains me to say this it's better for him to live without me," Quinn choked, feeling her heart breaking into a million pieces at the very notion of losing him after they just found each other.

Marta saw a pair of lights through the darkness with the first sign of early morning arriving right on time.

The van came closer before suddenly lifting off the ground in an explosion. It went five feet up and came back down with its wheels burning, the smell of rubber in the air. It happened suddenly without warning just before the bullets began raining down from every angle

"I don't know what the meaning of this is. We had an agreement. What went wrong? Again, I find myself adapting to present circumstances. You and I are getting on that boat. I have a bounty to collect." She motioned for her man to lay down cover fire while they made a run for it using the storm to shield them from being revealed too soon.

They ran into the driving wind with the gun pressed into Quinn's back from behind. She was showing her prisoner with actions there was no wiggle room for negotiation. They ran down the dock, people screaming in agony behind them.

Marta glanced back to see her men falling victim. At first, there was a pang of remorse but that changed to the greed of having all the money without having to share it. She could easily retire and travel the world making friends and lovers along the way.

"I'm not going to get any ideas. I think we can revisit what I suggested before you got that phone call. It's the only way you're going to save face and still collect." Quinn stepped onto the boat while it was swaying back and forth threatening to topple over.

The wind had died down significantly in the past few minutes.

"I never took the option off the table. I've always been about taking precautions. You have a deal." Marta nudged her captive into the boat before she fired up the engine and was moving away from shore within seconds.

"It looks like a war zone. Do you have everything you need to make this work? Don't concern yourself with me. I've given you everything with some discomfort." Quinn touched the missing tooth knowing she was going to need dental work from the finest oral surgeon money could buy to replace it.

"What we are doing is risky for both of us. I have my orders to turn you over to another boat on its way. I have a precise location. The storm is passing and I would say things are looking up." Marta was smiling and taking some time off would give her a chance to recharge her batteries.

She could retire but the work was too damn exciting to let somebody else have all the fun.

"I wouldn't say that," Bryce had emerged from below deck with a gun trained on Marta while putting his hand in front of Quinn in a protective gesture.

"I shouldn't have opened my big mouth. Do you want to tell him? I would hate to deprive you of seeing the look on his face." Marta didn't like surprises.

"You can lower the gun. Come with me and I will tell you everything. I would like to know what happened to you and the girls you went off with." Quinn had to reveal the plan and she showed him everything.

"Are you sure about this? I'm willing to concede on this issue. Whatever you decide is fine by me. I will follow your lead. To be devil's advocate, I would like to remind you how little her word holds weight with me." He remembered how the gun jammed when they overpowered the man until he was unconscious, tied up with a telephone cord like a prized calf at a rodeo.

"It's the only way I can think of to get them off my trail even if it is temporary. I'm glad to hear that you are on board with this plan." They held one another letting the silence feel like a breath of fresh air before a different kind of storm was coming.

"It was a simple matter of looking in his phone. We heard the location. That was more than enough to get the girls to work with me than against me. They were hell-bent on bringing the pain to the enemy. I hope they fared well. They were a pain in my ass but I had a soft spot for them," He swallowed and had to wonder what their fate would be after the dust settled.

The minutes ticked by with the boat jumping every few seconds when it hit a swell. They had arranged everything, including the scuba gear. It was going to be a close call and the timing was going to have to be perfect.

"It's been interesting getting to know you. The differences between us are minimal. I'm not sure what you would've done if the roles were reversed. It does pose the question of whether I can trust you. I know there is no honor amongst thieves. We are soldiers. Loyalty comes from the hardships we have suffered. It looks like we're going to find out what your word is worth. Come up here and keep your hands where I can see them. Bryce is to stay out of sight." She turned when the boat was slowing down to discover Bryce was no longer on board and one of the scuba tanks was missing.

"I didn't want him to be anywhere close to the excitement." Quinn walked up with her arms held high.

A spotlight from the other boat shined in her eyes.

A shadowy figure was directing the action. A man looking like he was in desperate need of a fix soon stepped forward with a metal black briefcase. His hands were trembling with his cheeks sunken.

Marta took a hold of the briefcase and received an elbow to her ribs. The gun went off between them while they struggled and she looked down to see the pool of blood in her hands.

She stared shocked at Quinn.

Quinn ran into the boat disappearing for less than two seconds when bullets rang out behind her. That was followed by an explosion lifting Marta backward still holding onto the briefcase splashing into the water and sinking below.

Mr. Rhodes wasn't pleased and screamed into the wind. His money was gone and the reason for the exchange had been blown into smithereens.

10

Ten

It wasn't what he was expecting, the explosion mirrored in his eyes. There was no way he could wait around forever when the spotlight was searching the area for any signs of survivors. That had been twenty-four hours ago.

Ironically, he was inside the villa next to theirs. It seemed only fitting to hide in plain sight where nobody would think to look for him. He had stood at the balcony all day waiting for any sign. The more time went by and his heart began to sink realizing he was alone.

The window of opportunity for her to use the scuba gear had closed fast. The explosion was bigger than expected with some of the debris whizzing by his head. He used the underwater tanks and light attached to make his way back to shore with barely enough oxygen before he had to hold his breath for the last 10 yards.

He remembered lying in the sand breathing deeply and looking at the sky. Nobody was around still in the mists of an extensive clean up after the hurricane. He wandered down the beach after stripping off the skin tight wetsuit.

He found his way back to the villa within an hour by following the path marked out.

Using the high powered binoculars left behind by Marta gave him a way to watch for anything out of the ordinary. It was getting to him. The waiting was the hardest part. Not knowing was making him age prematurely.

A sloshing sound caught him by surprise.

He turned to see the soaking wet form of Quinn. She dropped to her knees with a meek smile on her face.

"I thought I was never going to see you again," Bryce blurted out while lifting her to her feet and helping her to the bed.

"I wasn't expecting the explosion to be that big. I was hit pretty hard and my oxygen tank was ruptured. I was temporarily unconscious and almost drowned. I came to sputtering several yards away from what was left of the boat. There's no way to know if Marta survived. I wouldn't count her out." Quinn was still having problems breathing and collapsed, Bryce holding the back of her head until she was lying there looking at him.

"I'm just glad to see you. I know I have said this before but I think it needs to be repeated. I'm in love with you. I just wish you wouldn't keep using your nine lives. I would say you have less than two left and that's being conservative." Bryce could see the swell of her breasts through the transparent white T-shirt soaked and sticking to her skin.

"It's a good thing I know how to swim and hold my breath for long periods of time. Pacing my strokes was the only way I was going to make it back to shore," She shuddered at the feel of his fingers circling her nipples poking quite obscenely through the material.

"I don't want to wait. I have this way to get your temperature up," He teased before he bit into the T-shirt to make her growl in response.

"I would say this isn't the time but I don't see a better one. We have to take these moments and hold onto them. There's no way to know when our luck is finally going to run out. They think I'm dead. It's not like I haven't played this card before. I have to admit this time it was quite convincing and there was only a slim chance it was going to work out in my favor." Her words cut deep like a knife and she could see the fire burning out of control in his eyes.

"I'm tripping over myself to be with you. The touch of your skin and the look in your eyes lure me in until I can't sense the pain of losing you. We're going to reap what we sow in this life. I know we can make it out alive if we stand together." Bryce removed the t-shirt to see her glistening skin begging for his kisses.

Both hands cradled one of her breasts until he had a mouthful. His tongue circled the thick erasers with her hands above her head. She had her eyes closed to the pleasure he was inflicting on her. He had the war wounds physically and mentally from following her into the fire at the risk of getting burned.

"I don't know what I'm ever going to do without you and I hope I never find out. You have been amazingly patient even when I could see you had your misgivings about the plan. Trust like that is something I'm going to bottle for a rainy day. I make you one guarantee and you can take it to the bank. I have more to live for with you in my life. I was never much for making plans and going by the seat of my pants was a thrill beyond words. I will do everything in my power to make sure we are together for the long-term," She gasped between sentences with her eyes wide at the implication of what he was doing to her.

His hand slipped beyond the tightness of her shorts to feel how wet she was on the tip of his finger. The penetration was up to the knuckle and then another joined until there was three stretching her out making her yearn for something bigger.

She found her fingers occupied with something hot and thick blazing a trail in the palm of her hand. She squeezed and knew she had never felt like this before in her life.

Talking wasn't necessary when their actions spoke louder.

He made her rise from the mattress to strip her of her last defense. That bald mound was shiny and wet with her clit quite large and in charge. He lowered his head while gliding his fingertips down the side of her body to make her tremble. The salty discharge of the sea accompanied her natural scent to make him throb in her fist.

She saw his excitement straining against her nimble fingers. Taking him into her mouth encouraged a loud hum of approval. That feeling escalated what he was already doing by a million times. If she said she didn't like it, he would know she was lying through her teeth.

Her tongue moved over the empty space where one of her molars had been extracted. That tooth was meant to be found on the other boat along with the DNA evidence of her blood. They had no idea if Marta had finished her part of the plan before absconding with the cash pretending to drown in the aftermath.

A thrust had her gagging on the head and the first couple of inches. A mutual exchange of oral pleasure was a welcome greeting. She thought she was exhausted but the stirrings down below told her otherwise.

Their words were strangled by how they were busy satisfying each other's sweet tooth. The bed moved back and forth with the motion of the sexual ocean underneath them. The sheets were pulled from the four corners while she thrashed against his face giving him a different kind of milk mustache.

"I think you should stop and give me that cock," She urged when she came up for air with a sticky string of his nectar clinging to his cock head and her lip.

"A happy wife is a happy life," He mocked knowing there was no engagement ring on her finger.

He made her yelp when she found herself hanging upside down over the bed with all the blood rushing to her head. A firm insistent tug of her hips had his member surrounded by the heat of her warm juices. It was quite sudden and a piercing reminder of their devotion to one another. He stayed still inside her hot embrace staring down at her glazed over eyes looking up at him from the floor.

"It appears you are full of surprises. I guess there is an animal inside of you and I have the keys to the cage to let him out," She squealed when he began to move slowly back and forth with those lips kissing every inch on the way in and out.

Bryce loved the way that he was easing her pain. He could hear her voice crying out every time he bottomed out. It was a dysfunctional relationship but it worked for them in a way no other had.

"I know how to play this game by keeping things fresh. Doing it the same way all the time is going to get boring. Constantly changing things up will make you wonder what is going to happen next." He sat down with his legs dangling over the side still connected.

She felt his hands on her hips and then on her shoulders bringing her up to sit on top of him feeling a little lightheaded. Her hands slapped down on his chest pulling at the hairs while she bounded in the saddle like a runaway bronco.

"You really do know how to take my breath away. This body is always going to be yours. You have this uncanny ability to play my body like a musical instrument. There is no wasted motion. I can feel it coming," She stalled him by letting her arousal churn around the base of his equipment.

He could feel her grinding in a circle and knew from personal experience this was a woman's way to rub her clit at the same time. She was shining with this sexual sweat making them stick together like glue. They began moving together with their skin slapping together in musical harmony. It was giving them a chance to drift back in time when they first consummated the relationship.

She came with her fingernails scratching his chest leaving behind railroad tracks of her persuasion. Gasping and groaning while biting the bottom of her lip had her rhythmically squeezing the protruding invasion of his appendage.

This gave him a shot of adrenaline to turn her on her back with her legs over his shoulders. Pile driving his body down on top of her made her gasp with her legs spread in a wide arc. Her toes were pointed toward the ceiling with her inner thighs twitching.

"I have never known this kind of love before. I thought when most people talked about the concept it was all hype. A man like you can change a girl's mind," She screamed and was letting go of the pent-up sexual aggression bursting at the seams in her veins.

There were moments she hated every word coming out of his mouth and wanted to slap the taste from the smug expression on his face. She wanted to kiss him and wrap her hands around his neck. It had to be true love to have this unbalance of emotions fighting for control inside of her. Nobody could break her heart. He could with one look and didn't even know it. She wanted to keep it that way.

He was trying to wrap his brain around the feelings building with pressure between his legs. There was no way he could say it slowly with his temples throbbing, not including another muscle which was dangerously close to unleashing a white-hot storm.

She was convulsing underneath him and he could feel the inferno of her love tunnel drawing him to the inevitable conclusion. It wasn't just one orgasm and that moment of reprieve was soon punctuated by another one hot on the trail of the first one.

This was what was going to bring him to that moment of truth. His libido was struck with the match of her overwhelming orgasmic release. This brought forth a fountain of youthful expulsion with several strokes to feed it to her. They fell back exhausted and barely able to say two words to one another.

~~~

Mr. Rhodes had the evidence, and yet he was reluctant to walk down the hallway. It felt like the long green mile until he took a deep breath and opened the door.

"You have some explaining to do." A figure in a white shirt and pants to match was standing at the window with the sun on his face.

"It wasn't supposed to go like that. I went to an incredible expense to have the area searched for the past three days. There was blood on the hull and we found a tooth. I hate to be the bearer of bad news. The tests have come back to reveal they were Quinn's." He stood there nervous with the awkward silence almost enough to make him run from the room.

"I was a fool to think others without a vested interest could do my dirty work. Those bad habits came from you. You don't know my sister like I do. Like the phoenix, she will rise again from the ashes. This time I want you to dust off your old skills. You might be an old dog but you have many tricks yet to be played. I don't care how you do it. Find her and bring her to me. Don't come back without her," Harrison was the name given to him at birth but he had transformed into the hand of God.

Jehovah was what people called him. A Biblical revelation was coming.
~~~

Subscribe Now For Exclusive Content

Stay In Touch With LT To Receive Book Updates and Offers!

Sign up for my newsletter HERE
You can also join our ARC team HERE

Get in touch with L.T. by email at LTGrundyBooks@gmail.com

Subscribe now for exclusive updates, promos, giveaways, and updates on the next book!

A Note To You, The Reader

P.S. Readers:

Thank you so much for taking the time to read my book. Your feedback is very important to me. I'd like to ask a small favor. Would you be so kind as to click HERE and leave me an **HONEST** review?

Thank you so much!

Stay awesome,

L.T. Grundy

About the Author

L.T. Grundy lives with the love of his life Mary. They are the proud parents of two St. Bernards, Bella and Bastian. L.T and Mary enjoy outdoor activities like hiking and fishing, and anything else where the pups can tag along! Visit our Facebook page where you can connect with L.T.and sign up for our newsletter to receive offers and updates on when the next book will be released!

Also by L.T. Grundy

BLOOD IN
THE EYE OF
THE STORM
L.T. GRUNDY

TRAPPED BY
THE BLOOD
L.T. GRUNDY

BLOOD
RELEVATION
L. T. GRUNDY

www.ingramcontent.com/pod-product-compliance
Lightning Source LLC
LaVergne TN
LVHW052058160826
845678LV00015B/3288

* 9 7 9 8 3 7 3 9 5 8 1 4 1 *